Santa's Underwear

Written by **Marty Rhodes Figley** and Illustrated by **Marty Kelley**

It was Christmas Eve and time to get ready.

Santa shined his belt buckle and polished his best black boots.

He ate a healthy dinner to give him energy for the busy night ahead.

As Santa munched on his whole wheat bread, visions of delicious sweets danced in his head. Tonight children would leave tasty treats by their Christmas trees—just for him.

He brushed his teeth, then
scrub-a-dub-dubbed in the tub.

After blow-drying his hair, Santa combed his silky beard until it shined like the new-fallen snow.

Wrapped in his favorite robe, he admired
how jolly he looked in the mirror.

The hour had come to put on his special Christmas clothes.

Santa pulled open the underwear drawer in his dresser.

He poked around.

Where were his long, red, woolly undies?

Even though they were old, faded, and saggy, he always wore them under his suit on this special night.

They kept him warm as his sleigh soared across starry, wintry skies.

Santa looked through the
rest of the drawers...

checked the dirty
clothes hamper...

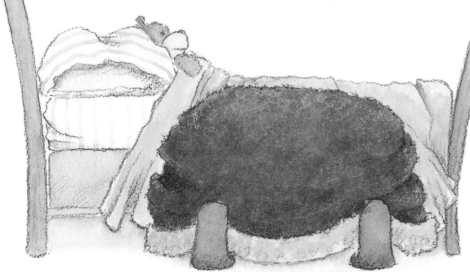

and peeked under
the bed.

But all he found there was one white sock, a dusty rubber reindeer toy, and two sticky candy canes.

No red undies!

Santa sighed.

"I guess this year I'll just have to wear something else."

He tried on the pink boxers and T-shirt Mrs. Claus had given him last Valentine's Day.

"Too many hearts and cutesy cupids!" he said.

Then he buttoned up the green long johns
he wore every St. Patrick's Day.

"These shamrocks aren't Christmassy at all!"

His Easter briefs, covered in pictures of dancing jelly beans, made Santa ask,

"What was I thinking?"

The tighty-whities and undershirt he'd bought for Thanksgiving were now a little too tighty and uncomfortable.

Well, he did eat a lot of pumpkin pie that day.

His boring, regular underwear just wasn't right for tonight.

What was he to do?

Wear no underwear at all on Christmas Eve?

That would certainly make him shiver and quiver out in the cold.

BRRRR!

Santa threw up his hands in despair.
The clock was ticktocking!

Children all over the world
were expecting their presents.

There was no time to waste!

He would just have to wear those silly shamrock long johns.
At least they were green...and warm.

Santa sighed as he opened the closet door to get his Santa Suit.

And there...

on a hanger...

RIGHT IN FRONT OF HIM...

tied with a bow...

were brand-new Christmas undies!

They were just like his old ones, but not saggy!

Their color was almost as bright as
Rudolph's nose!

A card tied to the front read:

Dear Santa,

Use this woolly gift tonight! Last Christmas we couldn't help but notice that you really needed some new undies!

Warm wishes,
Rudolph and the Reindeer Crew

"Ho! Ho! Ho!"

Decked out in holiday red, Santa admired
how twinkly his eyes looked in the mirror.

He finished dressing, plopped on his hat, and raced out the door.

As Santa hopped into his sleigh and rose out of sight, you could hear him exclaim, "Thank you, Rudolph, Dasher, Dancer, Prancer, and Vixen. Thanks to Comet, Cupid, Donner, and Blitzen! Now, let's get this show on the road! We've got a job to do!

Merry Christmas to you!"

With love, for Fenton, Dottie, Jasper, Annie, and Lulu—
my inspiringly delightful grandchildren.
MRF

*

This book is for Jay, Cris, Zach, Joey, Nolan, Maddie, & Aidan.
I hope aLL your Christmases are as warm and fuzzy as Santa's new underwear.

MK

Sleeping Bear Press®
2395 South Huron Parkway, Suite 200
Ann Arbor, MI 48104
www.sleepingbearpress.com

Printed and bound in the United States.

10 9 8 7 6 5 4 3 2

Library of Congress Cataloging-in-Publication Data

Names: Figley, Marty Rhodes, 1948- author. | Kelley, Marty, illustrator.
Title: Santa's underwear / written by Marty Rhodes Figley ; illustrated by
Marty Kelley.
Description: Ann Arbor, MI : Sleeping Bear Press, [2016] | Summary:
On Christmas Eve, Santa cannot find the special Christmas underwear
he wears every year, and nothing else seems quite right.
Identifiers: LCCN 2016007650 | ISBN 9781585369546
Subjects: LCSH: Santa Claus—Juvenile fiction. | CYAC: Santa Claus—Fiction.
| Underwear—Fiction.
Classification: LCC PZ7.F487 San 2016 | DDC [E]—dc23
LC record available at https://lccn.loc.gov/2016007650